My Trike

By Gina Ingoglia
Illustrated by Carolyn Bracken

A GOLDEN BOOK · NEW YORK
Western Publishing Company, Inc., Racine, Wisconsin 53404

ISBN: 0-307-10065-0/ISBN: 0-307-60065-3 (lib. bdg.)   B C D E F G H I J K L M

I have a red trike. This year I'm big
enough to ride it up and down the
block—all by myself!

I like to give my friends a ride. They hold on tight because I can pedal fast.

Sometimes a butterfly will land on
my handlebars while I'm riding.

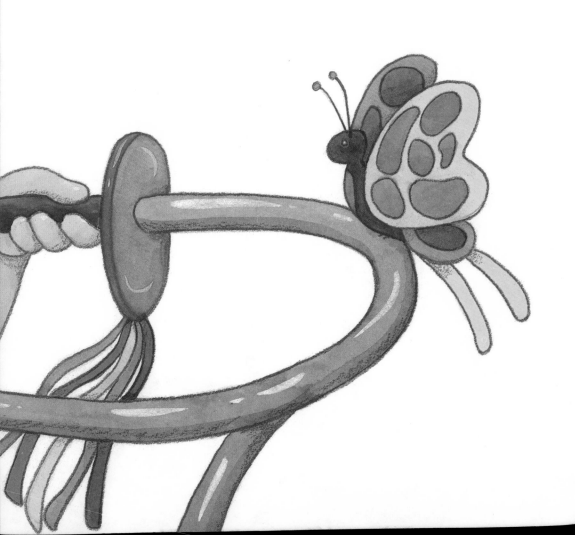

I wash my trike while Mommy and Daddy wash our car.

In summer, it's nice to stop and
have a cold drink in the shade.

I decorate my trike on the Fourth of July. My friends and I have our own parade.

I love to ride my trike through the sprinklers on very hot days.

In the fall, the leaves on the sidewalk crunch when I ride over them.

On Halloween, I'm a performing
bear who can ride a trike!

I have races with my friends up and down the block. I must be getting bigger, because I can win.

I have to take my trike indoors
when it's really cold and it starts
to snow.

I can hardly wait for next spring.
Then I'll be big enough to ride my
trike around the WHOLE BLOCK —
all by myself!